For dreamy girls and boys, the lifeblood of the world
— I. C. —

For Clare, Katherine and Laura
— P. B. —

Text copyright © 1988 by Ivor Cutler
Illustrations copyright © 1988 by Patrick Benson
First published in Great Britain by Walker Books Ltd.
All rights reserved. No part of this book may be reproduced or utilized
in any form or by any means, electronic or mechanical, including
photocopying, recording or by any information storage and retrieval
system, without permission in writing from the Publisher. Inquiries
should be addressed to Lothrop, Lee & Shepard Books, a division of
William Morrow & Company, Inc., 105 Madison Avenue, New York,
New York 10016. Printed in Hong Kong by South China Printing Co.

First U.S. Edition   1 2 3 4 5 6 7 8 9 10

Library of Congress Cataloging in Publication Data
Cutler, Ivor. Herbert : five stories / written by Ivor Cutler : illustrated by
Patrick Benson.   p.   cm. Contents: Herbert the chicken—
Herbert the elephant—Herbert the kangaroo—Herbert the question
mark—Herbert the Herbert. Summary: Each day is full of surprises for
a young boy as he wakes up and turns into a new animal.
ISBN 0-688-08147-9 : ISBN 0-688-08148-7 (lib. bdg.) [1. Animals—
Fiction. 2. Fantasy.] I. Benson, Patrick, ill. II. Title. PZ7.C978He 1988
[E]—dc19   88-2918 CIP AC

HERBERT
FIVE STORIES

HERBERT THE CHICKEN

HERBERT THE ELEPHANT

HERBERT THE KANGAROO

HERBERT THE QUESTION MARK

HERBERT THE HERBERT

Written by
IVOR CUTLER

Illustrated by
PATRICK BENSON

Lothrop, Lee & Shepard Books
New York

HERBERT THE CHICKEN

When Herbert woke on Monday, he found he had

become a chicken, and flew downstairs.

"Mom! Mom! I'm a chicken!" he squawked.

"That's nice, Herbert." She laughed and held up a mirror for him to look into.

Herbert laughed too. "Shall I go to school?"

"Why not?" said she, placing a dish of corn on the tablecloth. Clutching the rim with his claws, he pecked the plate clean, then flew upstairs for his satchel.

When he returned, his mother popped a plastic bag of corn into his brown canvas schoolbag.

"Peck a hole in it at lunch," she said, kissing his little yellow beak.

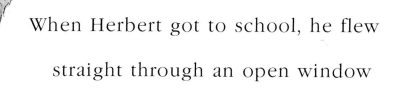

When Herbert got to school, he flew

straight through an open window

and sat on his seat. The class gasped.

"Sit down, everybody!" called Mr. Balloon,

the teacher. He turned to Herbert.

"Well, Herbert, you're a chicken."

Herbert flew around the room and

returned to his place. The class watched with

shining eyes and smiling lips, listening to the fluttering.

"Take out your diaries," said Mr. Balloon quietly.

The class started writing.

Herbert dipped his beak into a pot of Brown's ink

that the teacher placed by his feathers, and wrote:

Today I am a chicken.

It is lovely to be light.

I am very happy.

At playtime the children

gathered around in the playground.

"How did you become a chicken?" Annie asked.

But Herbert had no answer. "I just became one."

"Will you always be one?" Annie asked.

Herbert and Annie were in love.

He wagged his wings.

"I've no idea. I've never been one before."

The boys drifted away for a game of soccer.

Herbert joined them. They picked sides and Herbert

played center forward. He discovered that he

had a strong kick and scored three goals.

The other team said it wasn't fair, so he

switched sides and scored three goals for them.

Then the whistle blew and they

returned to the classroom.

Painting time.

Herbert posed on Mr. Balloon's head.

When they finished their paintings, the
children taped them to the wall.

What a large head Mr. Balloon had.

Then the lunch bell rang.

Herbert stayed in the classroom and pecked at his corn.

Annie kept him company, pecking

at her sandwiches.

"You look tired, Herbert," she said, peering at him.

"It's hard being a chicken," he sighed. "I think I'll

go home to bed. Goodbye, Annie,"

and, hovering, pecked her

lip slightly.

He flew slowly around the room for a last look, and then out the window. Annie watched him go until he was a dot (·), then sat at her desk and peeled an orange.

"I'm home!" clucked Herbert as he flew into his bedroom. Nobody was in, so he lay on the bed and went to sleep.

At five he woke and walked downstairs.

"Hey! I'm a boy again!" he called.

"A good thing!" said his mother. "It's boiled egg for supper."

And they both laughed.

HERBERT THE ELEPHANT

On Tuesday, very early, Herbert twitched the covers aside with his trunk and placed his feet down flat on the floor.

"What is happening?" cried his mother.

"I'm just getting out of bed," bellowed Herbert. "I'm an elephant."

"An elephant?" gasped his mom, racing upstairs. "Oh, Herbert, you'll break the house to bits. Come down as gently as you can."

"Don't worry, Mom. Mom, I can't get my trousers on."

"You're an elephant, Herbert. You don't need trousers. And when you come down, don't sit on a chair. Oh, my poor floors!"

She went down the stairs to the kitchen, took hold of the bread knife, and went out into the garden to cut long grass.

When she returned with a huge armful, her son was sniffing the kitchen.

"You know," he said, "this trunk is much better than my usual nose."

Then he settled down to the grass while his mother sat down to a cup of tea. She gazed keenly at his mouth as he ate.

Annie ran into the kitchen. "Hello, Mrs. Clockfoote!—Oh, Herbert. You're an elephant."

Herbert's mother handed Annie a large Granny Smith. Annie adored sour apples. They didn't give her a pain in the stomach.

"Come on, elephant. Bye-bye,

Mrs. Clockfoote. Thank you for

the apple," she said, and off they went.

Herbert curled his trunk around Annie's

waist and lifted her slowly onto his back.

"Go gently, Herbert, or I'll fall off,"

she called down.

When they reached the park, Herbert walked into
the pond and stood still in the middle. Annie stood
up and they sang "Baa Baa Black Sheep."

Then Herbert gently sprayed a trunk full
of water over four sparrows to give them a bath.

They sat on the grass while Annie ate
the apple with her mouth open.

Suddenly Herbert turned back into a boy.

"Oh no!" he yelled, and rushed under a bush.

"Annie, run home quickly,

please, and fetch my clothes.

I've nothing on!"

Annie burst out laughing and

handed him her sweater.

Then she ran at full speed

to Mrs. Clockfoote's (who laughed too). She was back in

no time and threw his garments into the bushes.

"Gosh, you're a terrific runner!"

called Herbert, as he dressed.

"Here's your sweater."

They returned home and ate a fried egg, baked

bean, and lettuce sandwich, with a big glass

of milk. Then they went to school.

"Today," said Mr. Balloon, their teacher, holding a

picture high, "we are going to talk about what

elephants do." And he smiled.

HERBERT THE KANGAROO

Herbert hopped out of bed and hit the ceiling.

"I'm a kangaroo!" he shouted down to his mother.

She laughed. "Did you nearly hurt yourself?"

"It's nothing to laugh at!"

he called crossly, then burst out

laughing. When his mother laughed,

it was like a disease. Everyone

else laughed too.

He hopped
downstairs as lightly as
he could, but the house shook.

"Herbert! Jump gently," said Mrs. Clockfoote,
staring with interest at her kangaroo son. Then she
pulled down a book on wild animals and looked to
see what he might like for breakfast.

She returned the book to the shelf, then
stepped into the garden with the bread
knife, and was soon back with a large
swathe of grass, which she
laid on the table.

Herbert jumped up and
tucked in, watched
by his adoring mom.

When he'd had enough, he turned to go upstairs for

his satchel, but Ermintrude Clockfoote stopped him.

"Let *me* go, Herbert, then the house won't fall down."

She returned in a jiffy, squashed the uneaten

grass into a brown bag, and kissed the tip of his nose.

Herbert hopped off.

"Hello, Annie!" he called as he passed her house.

"What a tail!" she exclaimed, running toward him. "My mom would have me sweeping the floor and dusting the ornaments if I had a tail!"

"So would mine if she thought of it," replied Herbert, though he knew he was clumsy and that Mrs. Clockfoote was scared to let him wash or dry the dishes.

"Sorry, Annie," said Mr. Balloon, the teacher, when they reached school. "No pets!"

"It's Herbert Clockfoote, and you know it." Annie smiled.

Mr. Balloon was great.

"It's me," said Herbert.

"All right, Annie, take your pet along
to the classroom," said Mr. Balloon.

Thud! Thud! Thud!
The principal's head
popped out of her door.
"What is it, Mr. Balloon?"
"It's our Herbert.
He's a kangaroo."
Mrs. Sack disappeared,
then popped her head out a second time.
"Mr. Balloon, I have a job for Herbert. Will you send
him to me with six strong children, please."
Mr. Balloon picked four girls and two
boys and sent them along with Herbert.
Mrs. Sack felt their arms.
"Come along," she said.

They walked along the tall corridor to the gymnasium and swung open the door. Mrs. Sack pointed to a large pile of thick jumping mats. "Take these outside and give them a good dusting."

The children carried the mats out, one between two, and dropped them all over the playground—even against the walls.

Then Herbert went to work.

He jumped on the mats as hard as he could and thwacked with his tail. He jumped sideways at those propped against the wall. Dust rose in such a cloud that it soon covered the school. Herbert was having the time of his life. Everybody coughed and choked. People in the street felt their way.

The six dirty children dragged in the clean mats, and Mrs. Sack gave them each a carrot. Herbert turned back into a boy just in time to get a carrot too.

When he entered the door after school, his mother handed him a cheese and onion and mustard sandwich. "Did you see the fog this morning?" she asked.

"Yes, Mom, I made it," he answered modestly, plunging the sandwich between his lips.

HERBERT THE QUESTION MARK

Herbert woke up and ran to the mirror.

"What are you, Herbert?" he asked.

"Mom!" he called, "I don't know what I am!" and scampered down to the kitchen.

"Nor do I." Mrs. Clockfoote frowned and shook her head. "What would you like for breakfast?"

"How do I know what to eat?" replied Herbert.

Ermintrude Clockfoote pointed her finger at the vegetable rack. "A potato! and a carrot! and a cabbage! and a parsley! and a leek!" Herbert pulled out the cabbage and kicked it across. She chopped off a slice and he gnawed it up.

Then she put on her hat and coat. "Come on, son, we're going to the zoo to find out what you are."

They walked to the bus stop and
jumped onto a bus.

"What's that?" asked the
conductor, pointing.

"Just what we want to find out," said Mrs. Clockfoote.

"Sorry, missus, he looks dangerous.

You'll have to get off."

Herbert ran up the

conductor's leg, then leaped

off the bus, followed by his mother.

The bus rolled away, with the

conductor, white-faced, shaking his fist.

Mrs. Clockfoote waved at a taxi to stop,
but the driver pointed to
Herbert, shook her head,
and drove on.

They walked back to the house
and Herbert's mom brought out
the old buggy. "Jump in,
my wee baby," she whispered.

She put a bonnet on his head, tying it under his chin.

When they reached the sidewalk, there stood

Herbert's sweetheart, Annie. Her eyes popped out.

"Have you got a new baby?" she gasped.

"Yes," said Mrs. Clockfoote. "Jump in and keep him

company. Now I have twins," she said,

and set off for the zoo.

On the way they all three sang,

"Baa baa black wool, have you any sheep?

No sir, no sir, two bags empty."

When they arrived, Herbert and Annie jumped

out and they all walked into the office.

"Good morning!" said Mrs. Clockfoote to the clerk.

"Can you tell me what this creature is?"

"Certainly, madam. It's a capybara, a South

American rodent. Look at those teeth. It's the biggest

rodent in the world. This one's only a baby."

"What does it eat?" inquired Mrs. Clockfoote.

"Juicy green plants."

"Thank you very much. Let's go, children!" She

smiled at the clerk and they returned

to the buggy.

Suddenly Herbert changed back to a boy.

"Aw!" said Annie sadly.

"What a waste!" said Herbert's mom.

"Jump in, Mom, and we'll give you a ride home," said Herbert.

Annie donned Mrs. Clockfoote's hat and coat, and
they headed for home, singing "Capybaras
eat juicy green plants" until they
ran out of breath.

HERBERT THE HERBERT

Herbert walked with Annie to the wood.

The secret path was black and curved.

There stood the big brown tree.

"What did you bring?" asked Annie.

Herbert pulled his schoolbag open.

"Lettuce sandwich, carrot, orange, and

a piece of ginger cake."

"I brought two cooking apples, a bottle of milk, a

soft-boiled tomato, a hard-boiled egg, and bread and

butter," said Annie. She slid through the big hole at

the bottom of the tree and disappeared. He could

hear her climbing, her sneakers squeaking up the

dark wood. Then there was silence.

Herbert followed, but when he squeezed up the

hollow tree, Annie was gone.

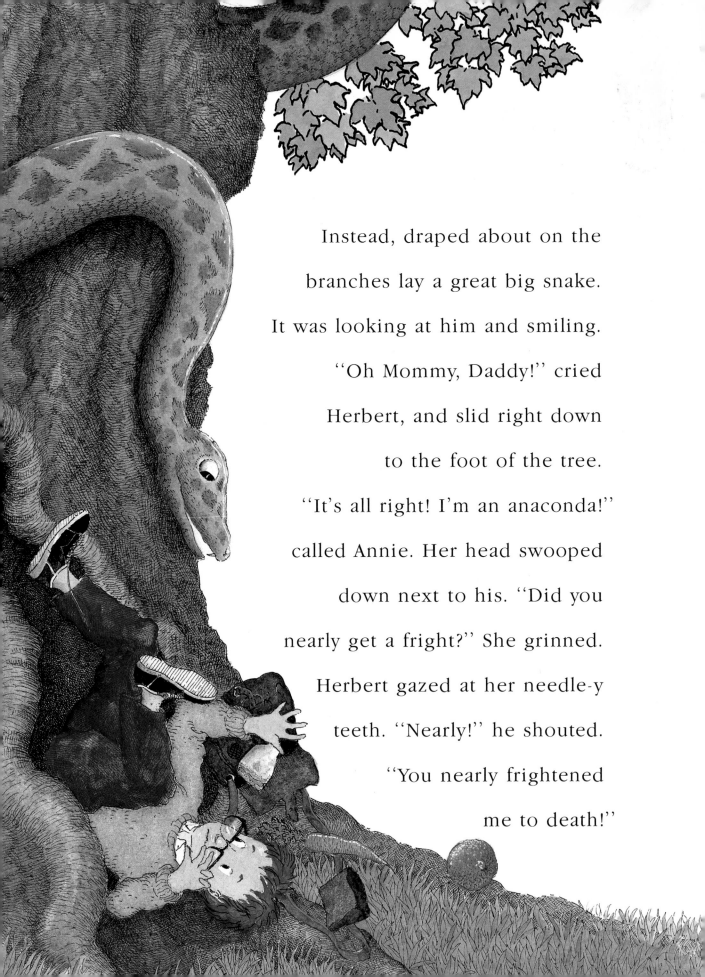

Instead, draped about on the
branches lay a great big snake.
It was looking at him and smiling.
"Oh Mommy, Daddy!" cried
Herbert, and slid right down
to the foot of the tree.
"It's all right! I'm an anaconda!"
called Annie. Her head swooped
down next to his. "Did you
nearly get a fright?" She grinned.
Herbert gazed at her needle-y
teeth. "Nearly!" he shouted.
"You nearly frightened
me to death!"

"There, I'll pull you back up,"
said Annie in a soft voice.
Grabbing a mouthful
of pullover, she hauled
Herbert to the top.
There was no room, so he sat
on a fat coil and ate his lunch.

Annie lifted her bag with the end of her
tail and dropped it with a little thud
down her large crimson throat.

Herbert's eyes followed the
bag as it made its way down
her body, getting smaller
and smaller as it went.
He felt it as it passed
under where he was sitting.

"Would you like

a slide, Herbert?" Annie asked.

Herbert sat himself on her neck

and slid down her body, which hung

out from the tree like a great branch.

Just at the last moment Annie flipped

her tail, and he flew up in the air.

She caught him with her teeth and

dropped him on her neck for

another slide.

"Stop!" begged Herbert,

after the eighth shot.

"I'm getting giddy!"

Annie set him on the ground,

then slid down beside him.

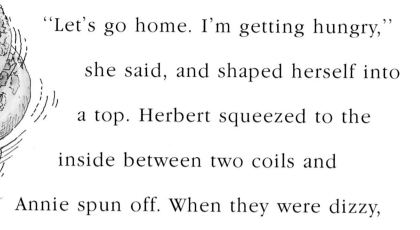

"Let's go home. I'm getting hungry,"
she said, and shaped herself into
a top. Herbert squeezed to the
inside between two coils and
Annie spun off. When they were dizzy,
Annie changed to a coiled
spring with Herbert lying
inside like a sausage
in a sausage roll.
Finally, she stuck her tail
into her mouth to become a hoop,

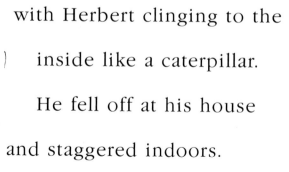

with Herbert clinging to the
inside like a caterpillar.
He fell off at his house
and staggered indoors.

"Mom! Come and see!
Annie's an anaconda!"

"Oh!" gasped Mrs. Clockfoote,
and ran out. She was just in time to
watch Annie change back to a girl—with a little soggy
schoolbag on the grass beside her.
Inside it lay an empty milk bottle.

"Goodbye, Herbert. Goodbye, Mrs. Clockfoote.
I want to tell my mom!" Annie waved
and ran off with her bag.

"And what were *you* this time?"
asked Mrs. Clockfoote.

"Me?" Herbert put a finger
on his chin and thought.
"I was a Herbert."